Mr. Zamboni's Dream Machine

A LORIMER BLUE KITE ADVENTURE

François Gravel

Mr. Zamboni's Dream Machine

Translated by Sarah Cummins

James Lorimer & Company, Publishers
Toronto, 1992

Originally published as *Zamboni*

James Lorimer & Company Ltd. acknowledges with thanks
the support of the Canada Council, the Ontario Arts Council
and the Ontario Publishing Centre in the development of
writing and publishing in Canada.

All illustrations by Frances Clancy, Toronto.

Canadian Cataloguing in Publication Data

Gravel, François
[Zamboni. English]
Mr. Zamboni's Dream Machine
Translation of: Zamboni.
ISBN 1-55028-403-7 (bound) ISBN 1-55028-402-9 (pbk.)
I. Title. II. Title: Zamboni. English.

PS8563.R28Z3613 1992 jC843'.54 C92-094858-8 PZ7.G72Za
1992

James Lorimer & Company, Publishers
Egerton Ryerson Memorial Building
35 Britain Street
Toronto, Ontario
M5A 1R7

Printed and bound in Canada

1

It's not easy being a goaltender. It takes me half an hour just to get dressed. First I put on my long underwear, then my socks, my shoulder pads, my chest pad, my throat protector, my pants. Then I have to wait till my dad is done talking with the coach so he can lace up my skates. They have to be really tight. When that's done, I lie down on my stomach so he can fasten my leg pads. By then I'm so weighed down I can hardly get back up. But that's not all: I still have to put on my sweater, my helmet, and my gloves. The game hasn't even begun yet and I'm already sweating.

Once I've got all my equipment on, my dad gives me advice: move out from the crease to cover the angles, don't be afraid to throw yourself down on the ice, and watch out for number 9, he's trouble. When my dad leaves, the trainer comes and sits down beside me. He tells me to stay inside the

crease, to stay on my feet as long as I can, and to watch out for number 12. I pretend to agree, but really I try to forget their advice. If I listen to all of it, I just get mixed up.

When the siren sounds, we hit the ice and then the real play begins. My heart's pounding, but as soon as the referee starts play, the only thing I worry about is the puck. A player gets around our defence and comes hurtling toward me. I get set. What will he do? Is it number 9 or number 12? Should I come out of the net to cover the angles or should I stay back in goal? There's no time to think about it — he shoots. Bam! on my leg pad. The puck falls in front of me. I can't let him get the rebound. I clear it with my stick and it goes into the corner. A player from my team tries to take it out, but he can't. The puck is still in our end and still dangerous. Parents are shouting in the stands. There's a crowd of players in front of me. I crouch to find the puck among all the legs and sticks. Suddenly I see it, right next to me. I flop down on the ice and stretch out my arm and cover the puck with my glove. The referee blows his whistle. Phew! The captain of our team taps his stick on my leg pad to congratulate me.

And the game goes on after that. The puck hits me in the stomach, the arms, the head, all over. Sometimes it hurts a bit, but not enough to bother me. I like the noise the puck makes when it hits my leg pads, my helmet, my stick, my chest pad, or the goal posts. I don't like the sound of it hitting the net behind me. But I can't work miracles. There's no such thing as a goalie who can stop every shot. Even Patrick Roy lets some of them get by.

I'm always surprised to hear the siren at the end. The game goes by so fast. We skate to centre ice and shake hands with the other team, then we go back to the dressing room. I always try to be the last one off the ice. That's because of Mr. Zamboni. That's not his real name, but I call him that because he drives the ice-cleaning machine. He's my friend. I really like him, especially since my grandfather died. He and I have a secret. When he drives his huge machine onto the ice, he waves to me. I wave back, then I go in to take my equipment off.

I really like being goalie. I like it a whole lot. Even when we lose. Even when the coach tells me everything I did wrong. The only thing I don't like is driving back home with my dad. I've got problems with him. That's why I've written this story. It's also why I made friends with Mr. Zamboni. But I can't tell the whole thing all at once. I'll start with my dad, and then the old man and how he showed me the inside of a Zamboni. It's pretty amazing, what's inside a Zamboni. Every kid should get a chance to see it. Not just goaltenders, not just hockey players. Everyone.

2

I said I had problems with my dad. I do. It's not that he's mean or doesn't take care of me or beats me or anything like that. I should also say that if you're only nine years old and you want to be a goaltender, you need a mother or a father. To lace your skates and fasten your leg pads, for sure, but also to carry the equipment. When my bag is full, it's so heavy that I couldn't even drag it to the arena. And the arena is so far from our house that we have to drive there. If I didn't have my dad, I wouldn't even be able to play hockey. That's why I have to listen to his advice. And that's my problem.

It's always the same thing. When he's driving me to the arena, he goes on and on about Ken Dryden, Vladislav Tretiak, and Jacques Plante. They were the goaltenders who played in his day. They didn't just tend goal, they also wrote books about it to help others. My dad reads all the goalies' books.

He knows them by heart. As soon as we get in the car, he starts to tell me what a good goaltender should do. I try to listen, but I usually can't understand what he's talking about because it's too complicated. Even when I do understand, it doesn't make any difference. Books are fine, but it's not the same in real life.

My dad smokes. He knows he should stop because it's bad for him. But I've known him for nine years, and he's still smoking. Whenever I ask him why he doesn't just stop, he tells me that it's easier said than done. I know exactly what he means. Sometimes I feel like reminding him that anyone can read a book by Jacques Plante and tell you what it says, but playing goal like Jacques Plante or Patrick Roy is not quite so easy.

My dad is always telling me that the most important thing in life is to get an education. But when I show him my report card, he hardly looks at it. He never has time to go to the parent-teacher meetings. But whenever there's a hockey tournament far away, he always has time. He's weird.

When we're coming home from the arena after our team has lost a game, he always says that the most important thing is to have fun. But he never has any fun. When we lose, he's scary. He tosses my bag into the trunk and tells me off for taking too long to get out of my equipment, he slams the car door, and he complains about everything. When we lose, there are too many red lights, too many bad drivers, and not enough sand on the road. When we win, he never complains about the red lights. You know my dad's problem? He's not consistent.

It's not half so bad when we win. Then he tells me about the spectacular saves he made when he was young. He played for the Junior Canadiens. He even almost played for the real Canadiens. He was chosen to be Ken Dryden's back-up, but he broke his ankle just before the first game. Then he had to have an operation, but the doctor botched it, and he could never skate again like before. Even now he can't skate because it hurts too much. If he had been able to keep on playing, he might have become the Canadiens' number one goalie,

and he could have written books giving tips on goaltending and he'd be rich. Instead, he had to go to work in a car factory. He could still write a book giving tips about motors, but he says he doesn't want to and no one would get rich doing that anyway.

He really has had bad luck. And it's true that I'm not as good a goaltender as he was. But sometimes I wish he'd remember that I'm only nine years old and that I'm not playing for the Montreal Canadiens, just the Sackville Novice C's.

3

Sometimes my mother takes me to hockey. Not often, only when my dad has to work late at the plant. If he really can't take me, he calls my mom. It's always a problem because she lives so far away. She lives with another man. I don't like him very much. He's some kind of scientist and he teaches at university. My mother met him when she went back to school. She said she had had enough of staying home all the time, so she took some courses at university, got a divorce, and now she has a new home. That was when I was in Squirts. I was seven then.

When my parents got divorced, I could have gone to live with my mother. I didn't want to, because of her new husband. He already has three kids of his own, so it was sort of complicated. Anyway, he might be a great scientist at the university, but my dad knows a lot more about motors and hockey.

My mom isn't very good at lacing up skates and fastening leg pads, but she does her best. When she's driving me back home to Dad's we never talk about hockey. She asks how I'm doing at school, how things are with Dad, stuff like that. When we get to the house, she checks to see if there's a light on, and then she lets me go. She never comes inside. It's better that way. Whenever my parents talk to each other, they always start fighting, and afterwards my dad is in a bad mood.

One time, when we were in the car, I told my mom that if Dad hadn't hurt his ankle, and if he had become the Canadiens' goalie, and if he had written a book and got rich, then she wouldn't have divorced him. She didn't answer, but I saw she was biting her lip. That's what she does when she feels bad, but doesn't want it to show.

4

One night we had a rough game against the St. Alban Tigers and we lost nine to two. It wasn't my fault. I got about two thousand shots on goal, and the St. Alban goalie only got two or three. Then the referee gave us penalties all the time for no reason. I couldn't wait for the siren to sound, but I was in no hurry to go into the dressing room, and I was especially in no hurry to drive home with my dad.

In the dressing room I knew the coach wouldn't say anything to me. When he's mad and wants to chew someone out, he always picks on Matteo, a defenceman. Matteo is his son. It's tough for Matteo. His dad played with the Junior Canadiens too.

Another kid with no luck at all is J.P., the centre. His mother always brings him to the rink. In the dressing room she's okay, even nice. Sometimes she brings us juice. But something happens to her when she sits in the stands. As soon as the puck is dropped, she begins to yell. I've never heard a voice like hers. She sounds like an opera singer who got her fingers slammed in the car door. You can even hear her over the horns and noisemakers. "Come on, J.P.! Both hands on your stick, J.P.! Go, J.P.! In front of the goal, J.P.!" Sometimes she yells so loud I wouldn't be surprised to see her come down onto the ice and play the whole game for us.

After the game was over, I looked up into the stands. My dad was all alone. He looked mad. I was in no rush to hear what I had done wrong so I took my time. I let all the other players leave the ice before me. As I was about to go, I heard a voice calling my name. It was Mr. Zamboni. He's an old man with white hair and a big white moustache and soft, sad eyes. I already knew him a bit because when I was little and playing in Squirts, my grandfather used to take me to the rink. Mr. Zamboni was a friend of his. When I went over to him, he got down onto the ice to talk to me. He told me I had played a good game and it wasn't my fault there were so many goals scored against us, and he said I deserved a little surprise.

I expected him to give me a piece of candy or some chocolate or something like that. But instead he opened a door on the side of the Zamboni and invited me to step in. I thought it was kind of strange, but I always like to look at machinery, so I went in.

It was dark inside, but I wasn't scared. There was a chair in one corner, like in a movie theatre. The old man told me to sit down and wait a while. He just had to adjust a few levers and then I could use his dream machine. His dream machine?

5

A dream machine is like a little movie theatre with just one seat. In front there's a screen that shows a movie, except that it's not a real movie with spaceships or bad guys. It's more like watching your own dreams on the screen. It's great.

In my first dream I was a goaltender. We were playing against the St. Alban Tigers. All the Tigers were shooting the puck at me, and I was blocking every shot. At the end I passed the puck to Yosuf, our team captain, and he scored and we won, one to nothing. Then when I was taking off my equipment in the dressing room, the coach of the Canadiens came to see me. He told me that all of his goaltenders were injured and he needed me to play that evening at the Forum against the Boston Bruins.

So I went to the Forum with my dad. He was really nervous and he kept giving me advice, but I knew that I would win. I had put special magnets in my glove and my leg pads to attract the puck.

When I got on the ice, I had to skate past the Bruins' bench. They all laughed at me because I was so little. They told me they would beat us 200 to nothing. But I knew they couldn't because of my special magnets.

Right after the opening face-off, a Boston player skated incredibly fast and deked the defencemen. He was all alone right in front of me. I didn't even have time to think what was happening. I stretched out my leg and made the stop. I smothered the puck, the referee blew his whistle, and all around me I heard a noise like an airplane taking off. It was the cheers from the crowd. Everyone in the Forum was yelling. I didn't know there could be that much noise. I don't think I could have even heard J.P.'s mother over all the racket.

We won that game two to nothing. I was chosen first star of the game, and the coach of the Canadiens asked me to stay on for the Stanley Cup playoffs. I said okay.

During the playoffs, I stopped all the best shots from Mario Lemieux, Steve Yserman, and Wayne Gretzky. When the Canadiens were ahead, I let a few shots in on purpose from time to time, just so no one would suspect anything.

My dad was really happy when we won the Stanley Cup. The next day he and I were in a parade through the streets of Montreal and all the papers had stories about me. Everyone wanted me to play against the Russians, but I said I couldn't go because my dad was waiting for me in the dressing room, to bawl me out.

I suddenly realized that I had been sitting in the dream machine a long time and my dad would be very angry. I hurried out as quickly as I could. The old man was surprised to see me.

"Are you leaving already?"

"My dad will be waiting and he'll bawl me out for being so slow."

"No, no, he won't. Take a look around."

I looked around and there were the players shaking hands at centre ice. Time had stood still while I was dreaming. It might have even gone backwards! But I decided I'd better head for the dressing room anyway. The old man told me there was nothing wrong with dreaming a little, it's good for you. He said I could come back whenever I wanted to.

On the way home, my dad got really ticked off at all the red lights and the other drivers who didn't know what they were doing. He was mad at me too. He said I had played badly and I should have listened to what he told me. I was thinking about the dream machine. Mr. Zamboni was right. It is good for you.

6

The next week we played the Gracefield Recreation Centre Hawks. We lost four to two, and I didn't play very well. It was because I kept thinking about the dream machine. As soon as I saw the Zamboni drive onto the ice, I went over. The old man opened the door and I went in and sat down. This time I was playing for Team Canada in a tournament in Moscow. We had the best players from the NHL on our team, and the best goalie in the world: me.

The tournament lasted two weeks. We played the Swedes, the Czechs, the Finns, the Americans, and the Russians. We won every game. My dad went with me everywhere and cut out my picture from the Moscow newspapers.

Then people took us around to all the museums and churches in Russia, and everywhere people asked me for my autograph. In Moscow we met Tretiak, the best Russian goaltender ever. My dad was thrilled to take a picture of Tretiak and me together.

When we got back to Canada, millions of people were waiting at the airport for my autograph, but I didn't have time because in real life we had lost four to two and my dad was going to be mad again.

That's the trouble with dreaming.

Driving back, my dad was in a really lousy mood. The worst thing is that we got into an accident just before we got home. It happened because the road was really slippery and the city workers hadn't put enough sand down. My dad braked, but the car kept on skidding and then we ran into a pole. We weren't hurt, but the car was a wreck.

I went to bed very early that night.

7

Things are starting to fall apart with my
dad. The accident has really changed him.
Sometimes when we're watching hockey on
television, it doesn't even make him happy
if the Canadiens win. When he's driving me
to the arena, he doesn't even give me advice
any more. He hardly says anything to me.

I guess it's partly my fault. We started the
season pretty well, but in the last two
months our team has hardly won at all.

Thank goodness for the Zamboni, or my
life would be miserable. After every game I
go and sit in the machine and dream about
hockey. After I've won all the Stanley Cups
in the world and all the gold medals, and
every championship in every sport, I dream
about other things. Sometimes I imagine
that I go see all the kings and presidents and
prime ministers and ask them to stop war
and to give money to poor countries. Other
times I dream that I'm a scientist and I in-

vent engines that run on water and don't pollute. But usually I dream that my mother and father get back together. They're both sitting in the stands and they're holding hands.

It's too hard to go back to the real world when the dream is over. I finally told the old man that I didn't want to sit inside the Zamboni any more. He was surprised, but when I told him why, he thought for a while and then he said that I was probably right.

I thanked him and went into the dressing room. The coach was in a pretty bad mood. He said that we lost because of Matteo, his son, but it was my fault too because I had my head in the clouds. I didn't like it when he said that in front of everyone. But I was in no hurry to leave and go home with my dad, especially since he had just got the car fixed and it had cost a lot.

When I came out of the dressing room, my dad wasn't there. Mr. Zamboni was there instead, and he told me my father was waiting for me in the car. He said he wanted to help me. I told him there was no point in dreaming. He said dreaming could help me to understand a lot of things and maybe even find some answers. But I didn't see how.

8

I went with the old man to a kind of garage where they keep the Zamboni when it's not being used. He told me to climb in, because he wanted to show me something.

I told him again that I didn't want to dream any more, because afterwards real life was too depressing. But then he explained to me that his machine could also travel through time and that he was going to show me something real.

Time travel? Count me in! I said I'd love to see the dinosaurs and maybe the Egyptians building the pyramids, but he said no. He twirled a few knobs and we travelled back to 1971, when my dad was playing with the Junior Canadiens. Not a bad idea to see that.

I settled into my seat. I couldn't wait to see all the spectacular saves my dad was going to make. The players weren't wearing helmets so it was easy to recognize them. I looked for Matteo's dad, but he wasn't there. Maybe he was injured that night.

Then I looked at the goaltender, but it wasn't my dad. I could tell that right away, even if he was wearing a mask. Maybe someone else was in the net because my dad was injured too? In front of me was a knob you could turn to see other years. I kept turning the knob and I saw hundreds of games played by the Junior Canadiens. My dad was never in any of them. Neither was Matteo's dad. I was a bit surprised, sure, but not as much as you would think.

To try and understand, I turned back to 1960. My dad was nine years old then and he was playing hockey at an outdoor rink. Everyone had skates except him. He was playing goalie anyway and his team was getting beat 14 to nothing.

When I left the Zamboni I understood a lot of things. The Junior Canadiens, the spectacular saves, the broken ankle — none of that was true. My dad has a dream machine too. But his dream machine is me.

9

When I turned the time-travel machine off, the old man came and sat down beside me. He flipped some switches and pressed some buttons, and the machine began to make a horrible noise. Lights flashed, smoke and sparks erupted from all sides, and the whole machine shook so much I began to get scared. I thought we were in a spaceship being attacked by extra-terrestrials.

"Now, Daniel," cried Mr. Zamboni, "now I will show you my very best invention!"

The Zamboni kept on making noise for a few more minutes, electrical wires started to sizzle, and then it settled down. A good thing too — there was so much smoke I was choking. When it stopped shaking, the old man turned some knobs and pushed some buttons and finally I found out what his invention was. It was a machine for making hot chocolate. He gave me a cup and then he started telling me about himself.

While I sipped the hot chocolate, he told me that he had been a Zamboni driver for nearly fifty years. He had seen thousands of hockey games and millions of fathers who told their sons they had played for the Junior Canadiens. That was why he had invented his machine. He figured that if the kids knew the truth, they wouldn't worry so much.

I drank my hot chocolate, which didn't taste very good. I thought to myself that maybe his inventions weren't as wonderful as he thought they were.

When he finished talking, I told him that his machine had helped me understand a lot of things that I wished I had never known about. What good does it do to find out the truth, what's the point of dreaming if nothing ever changes?

He answered that sometimes dreams do come true. Besides, you have to dream if you're ever going to do something important. Sure! That's easy to say.

For two weeks I thought about what Mr. Zamboni had said. I wondered what I could do to make my dreams come true. I didn't have enough money to go see all the presidents, kings, and prime ministers in the world and tell them to stop their wars. Anyway, I'm not sure they would have listened to me. Should I invent an engine? First I would have to buy some metal and my dad would have to take me to the factory with him. I knew he wouldn't want to. Every time I want him to take me to the factory, he says the boss wouldn't like it because of insurance. I don't know what insurance is, but I don't think it's a very good invention. Should I become the best goaltender in the world? Easier said than done.

One night, I was in the dressing room getting changed, and suddenly I noticed J.P. sitting on the bench across from me. His mother was tightening his laces and giving him advice non-stop. The more I looked at J.P.'s mother, the more she reminded me of my father. She probably needed a dream machine too. When I thought about the dream machine, I remembered the time I had met J.P.'s mother in the video store. She was renting a war movie for J.P. and a love movie for herself. She looked very pretty in her fur hat. She has beautiful eyes and she smelled good. The strange thing, though, was that she seemed so quiet and gentle, not at all like she is in the stands. Parents are never consistent. It all depends on where they are.

Anyway, soon after that, something strange happened. Maybe Mr. Zamboni's machine really could make dreams come true. Although not quite the way you expected.

11

The next Saturday, my dad had to work at the factory and my mom was out of town with her scientist. I had arranged with J.P. for his mother to pick me up and drive us both to the arena. After the game I was invited over to their house for dinner. My dad was supposed to come pick me up at a quarter to eight.

We played the Knights that day. They were a good team, but we had been working really hard and we managed to tie them. J.P. scored a goal and I made two fantastic saves, so everybody was happy.

J.P.'s mom made spaghetti for dinner. It was really good. After dinner J.P. and I went upstairs to his room. We played on the computer for a while. When my dad rang the doorbell, we were just beginning a game of chess.

J.P.'s mom started out by saying that I had been very nice and J.P. and I got along

together very well. My dad seemed a bit embarrassed. He called out to me and said it was time to go, but I asked if I couldn't just please finish my chess game. Since I had asked so politely, he had to agree. Then J.P.'s mother offered him a cup of coffee since it was so cold outside, and he said yes.

J.P. and I were involved in our chess game, but we were also listening to every word they said. Maybe we played a little slower on purpose. It takes grown-ups a long time to make friends.

First they discussed the hockey game. J.P.'s mom said I had played very well, so my dad was happy. He said he thought J.P. had a lot of talent, so then she was happy.

Then they talked about the Canadiens. My dad was surprised to learn that J.P.'s mom knew the statistics on all the players. At eight o'clock we still hadn't finished our chess game, so J.P.'s mom turned on the television.

That evening we stayed until the end of the second period. The Canadiens were leading Boston four to nothing. It might have been a coincidence, but I couldn't help thinking that the Canadiens were playing extra well just so that we could stay a bit longer. At ten o'clock, we had to go so that I wouldn't get to bed too late.

In the car on the way back home my dad didn't talk about Ken Dryden. Instead he asked me all kinds of questions about J.P.'s mother. Had she been divorced long? Did I think she was nice? Would I like to invite J.P. over next week?

12

Lately things are going much better with my dad. When he drives me to the arena, he still talks about Ken Dryden and Jacques Plante, but he's not talking to me. He's talking to J.P.'s mother. They sit in the front seat and they talk about hockey all the time. J.P. and I sit in the back seat and listen to them. It's funny because my dad never talks about when he was goalie for the Junior Canadiens any more.

When we get to the rink, they go sit in the stands right away. J.P. and I have decided we're old enough to do up our own laces. J.P. is playing a lot better now that his mother has stopped yelling. He doesn't worry all the time about making a mistake. I'm playing better too. If a shot gets by me, I just try to forget about my dad instead of worrying about what he'll say.

There are two more games before the playoffs. Our trainer says we've got a

chance. It was a tough season, but lately the team has been doing well. You never know — maybe we'll win the novice championship. I'd like that. But even if we don't win, it's not the end of the world. My dad will be in a good mood anyway when we get home.

On Sundays when the weather's nice, all four of us go skating together. My dad doesn't skate very well. Sometimes we have races. J.P. always wins, I come in second, and our parents are far behind. I think they skate slow on purpose. It's because they want to talk.

J.P. and I think our parents are going to get married. But maybe not. Grown-ups always take a long time to make up their minds.

Last week they took us to the Forum to see a real Canadiens game. When we got back to J.P.'s house, I was tired so my dad said I could sleep over. He told me he would come get me in the morning.

The next morning when I got up, my dad was having breakfast. He looked a little embarrassed but he was in a good mood.

I like J.P.'s mother. She's not like my own mother, but I'm getting used to her. When I go see my real mother, she seems happy that things are working out for Dad. They hardly ever fight when they talk on the phone now.

Sometimes I think about what I'll do when I grow up. My dream is to become goaltender for the Canadiens. When I told my dad that, he said there's no point in dreaming. Maybe he's right.

If I never become the Canadiens' goalie, that's all right too. After all, there are a lot of other things I could do. I could invent engines that don't pollute, I could go and help poor countries by building dams or digging wells, there's all kinds of interesting things I could do. But what I'd like best of all is to become goaltender for the Canadiens. And if I don't, I think I'll take a course to learn how to drive a Zamboni.

About the author
Born in Montreal in 1951, François Gravel
has written five novels for adults—*La note de
passage*, *Benito*, *L'Effet Summerhill*, *Bonheur
fou*, and *Les Black Stones*. In addition to *Mr.
Zamboni's Dream Machine*, he has written
three novels for young people—*Corneilles*,
Granulite, and *Deux heures et demie avant
Jasmine*, which won the Governor General's
Award in 1991. François Gravel teaches in
Montreal.

About the translator
Sarah Cummins has translated many
children's books. Among them are *Maddie in
Goal*, *The Swank Prank*, and *The Amazing
Adventure of Littlefish*. She is preparing a
doctorate in French linguistics.